Sneaky Deals
and Tricky Tricks

Retold by Rose Impey

Illustrated by *Louise Voce*

ORCHARD BOOKS

Other titles in this series:

Bad Bears and Good Bears

Bad Boys and Naughty Girls

Greedy Guts and Belly Busters

Hairy Toes and Scary Bones

I Spy, Pancakes and Pies

If Wishes were Fishes

Knock, Knock! Who's There?

Over the Stile and into the Sack

Runaway Cakes and Skipalong Pots

Silly Sons and Dozy Daughters

Ugly Dogs and Slimy Frogs

ORCHARD BOOKS
96 Leonard Street, London EC2A 4XD
Orchard Books Australia
14 Mars Road, Lane Cove, NSW 2066
First published in Great Britain in 2000
First paperback publication 2000
Text © Rose Impey 2000
Illustrations © Louise Voce 2000
The rights of Rose Impey to be identified as the author
and Louise Voce as the illustrator of this work
have been asserted by them in accordance with the
Copyright, Designs and Patents Act, 1988.
A CIP catalogue record for this book is available
from the British Library.
ISBN 1 86039 973 8 (hardback)
ISBN 1 86039 974 6 (paperback)
1 3 5 7 9 10 8 6 4 2 (hardback)
1 3 5 7 9 10 8 6 4 2 (paperback)
Printed in Great Britain

1. This book ~~~~~~ t three weeks. It is to be
   r~~~~~ last date stamped below.
   ~~~~~ arged for every week or
   ~~~~~ erdue.

2 6 NOV 2001	1 6 JUN 2004
– 5 MAR 2002	1 2 JUN 2006
1 5 MAR 2002	
2 7 MAR 2002	
2 4 APR 2002	
1 8 MAY 2002	
1 2 JUN 2002	
2 5 SEP 2002	
2 5 NOV 2002	
– 3 FEB 2003	
2 8 MAR 2003	
1 1 SEP 20??	

★ CONTENTS ★

A Deal's a Deal and That's That

Coyote thinks he's such a fine fellow.
Always showing off, always trying
to eat the smaller animals. Here he
comes now, swaggering along.
Watch how Bear tricks him and
teaches him a lesson he won't forget.

"My dear friend, Coyote," says Bear, "how would you like to do some farming with me? If we share the work, we'll only have half as much to do."

Hmmm, Coyote likes that idea.
They can share the crops too,
he says.

Bear's already thought of that. He tells Coyote, "One of us can take what grows *above* the ground, the other can take what grows *below*. You can choose first."

"*Hmmm*," says Coyote, "I choose tops."

"Sounds good to me," says Bear. "Then I'll have bottoms."

The two friends shake on it, to show it's a deal.

"No going back on a deal,"
says Bear. He grins, but he doesn't
let Coyote see him grinning.

Coyote and Bear work really
hard. They plant a whole field of
potatoes. They weed them,

water them,

hill them up.

Then they wait until they grow.

In the autumn, Bear says to Coyote, "Time to pick our crops."

But when Coyote gets to the field, what does he find? Bear's already dug *his* potatoes out of the ground.

All that's left for Coyote is the tops. And you can't eat those.

Coyote's mad; he's bubbling like a pot of stew. But what can he do?

A deal's a deal and that's that.

Well, come the next year Coyote's ready. He won't be tricked again.

"This time," he says, "*I'll* take the bottoms and *you* can take the tops."

"Sounds good to me," says Bear. And the two friends shake on it, to show it's a deal.

"No going back on a deal," says Bear. He grins, but he doesn't let Coyote see him grinning.

Coyote and Bear work hard in their field. They plant a crop of wheat that grows up towards the sun, thick and golden.

At last it's time to pick the crop.
But when Coyote gets to the field,
what does he find? Bear's already
cut the wheat and taken his share.

All that's left for Coyote is the
stubble and roots. And you can't
eat those.

Coyote's mad; he's buzzing like a wasps' nest. But what can he do?

A deal's a deal and that's that.

Now Coyote's learnt his lesson.
He tells Bear, "You won't catch
me a third time. This time I'll take
the bottoms *and* the tops."

"Won't be anything left for me,"
says Bear, "if you take the bottoms
and the tops."

"Guess you'll have to make do with the middles," says Coyote, chuckling.

"Sounds good to me," says Bear. "Let's shake on it. Remember: a deal's a deal and that's that."

Coyote and Bear work hard
planting a whole field of sweetcorn.
They weed it and water it and
then they wait for it to grow.

The sun shines and the rain
comes down and that crop of
sweetcorn grows tall and strong.

At last it's ready to pick and here comes Coyote with his wheelbarrow. But what's this?

Bear has already cut down the plants. He's left the tops and the bottoms for Coyote, but you can't eat those.

He's taken all the sweetcorn that
grows in the middle. And you can
eat that!

This time Coyote's fit to *explode*.
But what can he do?

"A deal's a deal and that's
that," says Bear, grinning.
He doesn't care who sees him
grinning now. He's got the
sweetcorn. All of it.

Coyote has surely learnt his
lesson this time. He creeps home
with his bushy tail between his
legs, all the other animals
laughing.

"No more farming," he says.
"Never again. No more deals
for me."

Coyote worked hard,
but he didn't get fat,
because a deal's a deal,
and that's that!

★ The Tug of War ✩

There surely is nothing Brer Rabbit
likes better than playing tricks.
Watch him trick Brer Elephant
and catch Brer Whale by the tail.

But first, listen to the two of
them bragging about how big
and strong they are.

"Oh, Brer Whale, you are
the biggest, strongest animal in
the sea," says Brer Elephant.

"And you, Brer Elephant, are the biggest, strongest animal on land," says Brer Whale.

"If we joined together," says Brer Elephant, "we could rule the whole world."

Hmmm, Brer Whale likes the sound of that.

But Brer Rabbit doesn't like the
sound of it. "No one's going to
rule over me," he says.

He thinks of a clever plan to teach those two a lesson. First he makes a strong thick rope, then he goes to find Brer Elephant.

"Well, good morning to you, Brer Elephant," says Brer Rabbit, oh-so-polite. "Which of us do you think is stronger?"

Brer Elephant isn't polite. He
sprays water all over Brer Rabbit.
"I'll show you who's stronger," he
says, "by trampling you under
my foot."

"Oh, no," says Brer Rabbit quickly. "Don't do that. Let's have a tug of war instead."

Brer Elephant agrees to a tug of war and he wants it right now.

"Here's the rope," says Brer
Rabbit. "Tie it round your leg
while I get ready. But don't start
till I give three sharp tugs, then
just try your best."

Brer Rabbit runs *skipperty-lipperty* as fast as he can to find Brer Whale.

Brer Whale is floating in the water near to the shore. Brer Rabbit calls out, oh-so-polite, "Well, good morning to you, Brer Whale. Which of us do you think is stronger?"

Brer Whale isn't polite either.
He sends up a huge spout of water.
It wets Brer Rabbit through.

"A whale is stronger than a million rabbits," he says. "Shall I show you how easily I could swallow you up?"

"Oh, no," says Brer Rabbit quickly. "Don't do that. Let's have a tug of war instead."

Brer Whale agrees to a tug of war. So Brer Rabbit tells Brer Whale to come close to the shore, then he can tie the end of the rope round his tail.

"Whatever you do," he tells Brer
Whale, "don't start till I'm ready.
I'll give three sharp tugs, then just
try your best."

Brer Rabbit runs *skipperty-lipperty* deep into the forest until he's hidden. Then he gives three sharp tugs on the rope and stands well back.

Brer Whale starts to pull. Brer
Elephant starts to pull. Soon the
rope is stretched tight.

They're both pulling as hard as
they can, but nobody's winning.

Suddenly, Brer Whale gives an extra big pull and shoots forwards in the water.

Brer Elephant starts to slip and
slide backwards through the forest.

"That Brer Rabbit is stronger
than I thought," he pants.

Brer Elephant wraps his trunk
around a tree and digs his four
huge feet into the ground.

Then he pulls and he pulls and he...pulls.

Brer Whale feels the rope
tugging on his tail. He stops
swimming forwards and suddenly
he's swimming backwards.

"That Brer Rabbit can certainly pull," puffs Brer Whale. He fills his lungs with air and swims as hard as he can.

Brer Whale and Brer Elephant are both so strong that first one moves forward, then the other pulls him back. Neither of them will let a scrawny little rabbit beat him.

They both pull

and pull
and...pull!

This tug of war could go on all day, and it would go on all day, but watch this! Brer Rabbit has one more trick up his sleeve. He takes his knife and cuts clean through the rope. *Slish! Slash!*

"Help! Oh, help!" roars Brer Whale. He turns a huge somersault and lands in the water with a big belly-flop.

"Owww!" yells Brer Elephant.
He runs – *smack! bang!* – into a
tree and almost knocks himself out.

And what about that trickster
Brer Rabbit? He just runs away,
laughing as loud as he can.

Whale roars, "Help! Oh, help!"
Elephant yells, "OWWW!"
Rabbit wins the tug of war.
End of story now.

Trickster tales are found in many parts of the world but they are especially common in America, where *A Deal's a Deal and That's That* comes from, and the Caribbean, where *The Tug of War* originates. Brer Rabbit is one of the most famous tricksters in the world of stories.

Here are some more stories you might like to read:

About Tricks and Tricksters:

Tricky Tortoise
by Mwenye Hadithi
(Hodder Children's Books)

The Tortoise, the Monkey and the Banana-Tree
from *A Treasury of Stories for Seven Year Olds*
chosen by Edward and Nancy Blishen
(Kingfisher)

About Trials of Strength:

Odon the Giant
from *Nursery Tales from Around the World*
retold by Judy Sierra
(Houghton Mifflin)